BENJAMIN RABBIT

AND THE

BAD DREAM

Written by
Irene Keller

Illustrated by
Dick Keller

Ideals Publishing Corporation
Nashville, Tennessee

Text copyright © MCMLXXXVI by Irene Keller
Illustrations copyright © MCMLXXXVI by Dick Keller
All rights reserved. Printed and bound in U.S.A.
Published simultaneously in Canada.

ISBN 0-8249-8153-7

Benjamin Rabbit will always remember that special Saturday night—the night before his best friend, Harold Hopalong, moved away. Because it was such a special occasion, the two little rabbits were allowed to stay up late.

Benjamin and Harold had a great time—lots of fun and lots of treats. They nibbled on candy bars and carrot cake. They ate mounds of jelly beans and they drank soda pop.

They even watched a scary movie on television.
When Harold went home late that night, Benjamin didn't feel too well. He crawled into bed with

his head full of horrors and his tummy full of candy bars and carrot cake and jelly beans and soda pop. In no time at all, Benjamin was dreaming.

He dreamed he was running and jumping with
Harold in a lovely field of sweet clover. They were
having a wonderful time, hopping higher and higher,

when—all of a sudden—Harold hopped so high that
he disappeared! Harold just vanished! And Benjamin
was all alone in the meadow.

The next thing he heard was a big loud *ROAR* and a *THUMP, THUMP, THUMP.* Benjamin felt the ground shaking beneath him. Then, behind the hedge, a horn appeared! Then a huge head! And a giant hump! It was a monster. *A MONSTER!*

Benjamin got such a fright that he woke up.

It was still dark in his room. Benjamin knew it was just a bad dream but he was still scared. He decided he'd better make sure that the monster hadn't followed him home.

Benjamin looked under his bed. Nothing there!
Then he looked behind the curtains. Nothing there!
Then, very slowly, a teeny tiny bit at a time,
Benjamin opened his closet door, and there it was—

large as life! A monster as big as a house with one huge red eye right in the middle of its forehead. And it was looking right at Benjamin!

Benjamin ran to his mother's room as fast as his legs could carry him.

"Mother! Mother!" he yelled. "Wake up! There's a monster in my closet. It's as big as a house and has one huge red eye in the middle of its forehead."

"Oh, Benjamin, you've had a bad dream," said Mother Rabbit. "I'll get my can of Monster Mover and spray your closet."

"No, no!" said Benjamin. "The Monster Mover won't work this time. This is a *real* monster. I better sleep in your bed tonight."

"Well, first let's have a look," said Mother Rabbit, putting on her robe and slippers.

Benjamin hid behind Mother Rabbit as she went
into his room.

The minute Mother Rabbit opened the closet

door, Benjamin dived into his bed and pulled the covers over his head.

"Oh, no!" he yelled. "I can't look."

Mother Rabbit gave a little giggle.

"Come here, Benjamin, and see your Closet Monster," she said.

Benjamin peeked into the closet and there it was

again! A monster as big as a house with a huge red eye in its forehead.

"EEEEEK!" Benjamin yelled and hid his face.

As Mother Rabbit switched on the closet light, she said, "Look again, Benjamin."

Benjamin peeked again and this time the monster was gone.

"Where did it go?" asked Benjamin.

Mother Rabbit laughed and pointed to an old

bicycle reflector on the top shelf of his closet.

"See?" said Mother Rabbit. "It wasn't a monster. It was only the moon shining on your bicycle reflector. It just looked like a big red eye."

Benjamin laughed, too, but he was still shaking.

"Just to make sure," said Benjamin, "will you spray the closet with your Monster Mover anyway?"

"Of course I will," said Mother Rabbit.

"Funny," said Benjamin Rabbit. "That Monster

Mover smells just like air freshener to me."

"Yes, but not to Closet Monsters," said Mother Rabbit. "Now let's have a nice glass of milk before we go back to bed."

The kitchen was warm and cozy. Benjamin
started to feel better.

"Where do bad dreams come from?" he asked
Mother Rabbit.

"Sometimes we get bad dreams when we eat too much of the wrong thing," said Mother Rabbit.

"I did that," said Benjamin, remembering the candy bars and carrot cake and jelly beans and soda.

"And sometimes we get bad dreams if we watch a show that is too scary," said Mother Rabbit.

"I did that, too," said Benjamin, remembering the scary movie.

"And sometimes we get bad dreams when we are worried or afraid of something," said Mother Rabbit. "And in that case, Benjamin, it helps to talk about it. Maybe we should talk about your dream."

"The bad part of my dream began when Harold disappeared and I was all alone in the meadow," said Benjamin. "And Harold is moving away tomorrow."

"I know you'll miss Harold," said Mother Rabbit. "But just because he's moving away doesn't mean he's going to disappear from your life. Harold will still be your friend, even if he lives somewhere else."

"But Harold is such a good friend," said Benjamin sadly.

"And *you* are a good friend, too, Benjamin," said

Mother Rabbit. "And because you know how to be a good friend, you will have many, many friends in your lifetime."

Benjamin began to feel sleepy.

"Can we go and visit Harold soon?" he asked his mother as she tucked him into bed.

"Of course we can," said Mother Rabbit. "And now it's time to say good night, Benjamin."

"And sweet dreams!" said Benjamin Rabbit.